STAR WARS®

DARTH VADER AND THE LOST COMMAND

VOLUME FOUR

SCRIPT
HADEN BLACKMAN

PENCILS
RICK LEONARDI

INKS
DANIEL GREEN

COLORS
WES DZIOBA

LETTERING
MICHAEL HEISLER

COVER ART
TSUNEO SANDA

Darth Vader has been sent to the Atoan system, within the mysterious Ghost Nebula, to locate a missing Star Destroyer and its commander, Admiral Garoche Tarkin—Moff Tarkin's son.

With the assistance of Lady Saro, the system's religious leader, the missing admiral was tracked to a floating city on a planet of boiling tar. Vader and his second in command—Captain Shale, a personal friend of the admiral—led an attack on the city.

Having captured the floating city, Vader uncovered allegations that the still-missing Garoche Tarkin was a traitor. That night, during an uneasy sleep, Vader dreamed of Padmé, who gave him a warning. Vader woke to find Captain Shale's storm commandos in his quarters . . .

The events in this story take place approximately nineteen years before the Battle of Yavin.

DARK HORSE COMICS

Spotlight

visit us at www.abdopublishing.com

Reinforced library bound edition published in 2012 by Spotlight,
a division of the ABDO Group, PO Box 398166, Minneapolis, MN 55439.
Spotlight produces high-quality reinforced library bound editions for schools and
libraries. Published by agreement with Dark Horse Comics, Inc., and Lucasfilm Ltd.

Printed in the United States of America, North Mankato, Minnesota.
102011
012012

 This book contains at least 10% recycled materials.

Library of Congress Cataloging-in-Publication Data

Blackman, W. Haden.
 Star wars : Darth Vader and the lost command / script, Haden Blackman ;
pencils, Rick Leonardi. -- Reinforced library bound ed.
    p. cm.
 ISBN 978-1-59961-980-4 (volume 1) -- ISBN 978-1-59961-981-1 (volume 2) --
ISBN 978-1-59961-982-8 (volume 3) -- ISBN 978-1-59961-983-5 (volume 4) --
ISBN 978-1-59961-984-2 (volume 5)
 1. Graphic novels. 2. Science fiction. I. Leonardi, Rick. II. Title.
 PZ7.7.B555Ssm 2012
 741.5'973--dc23
                          2011033322

All Spotlight books are reinforced library binding
and manufactured in the United States of America.

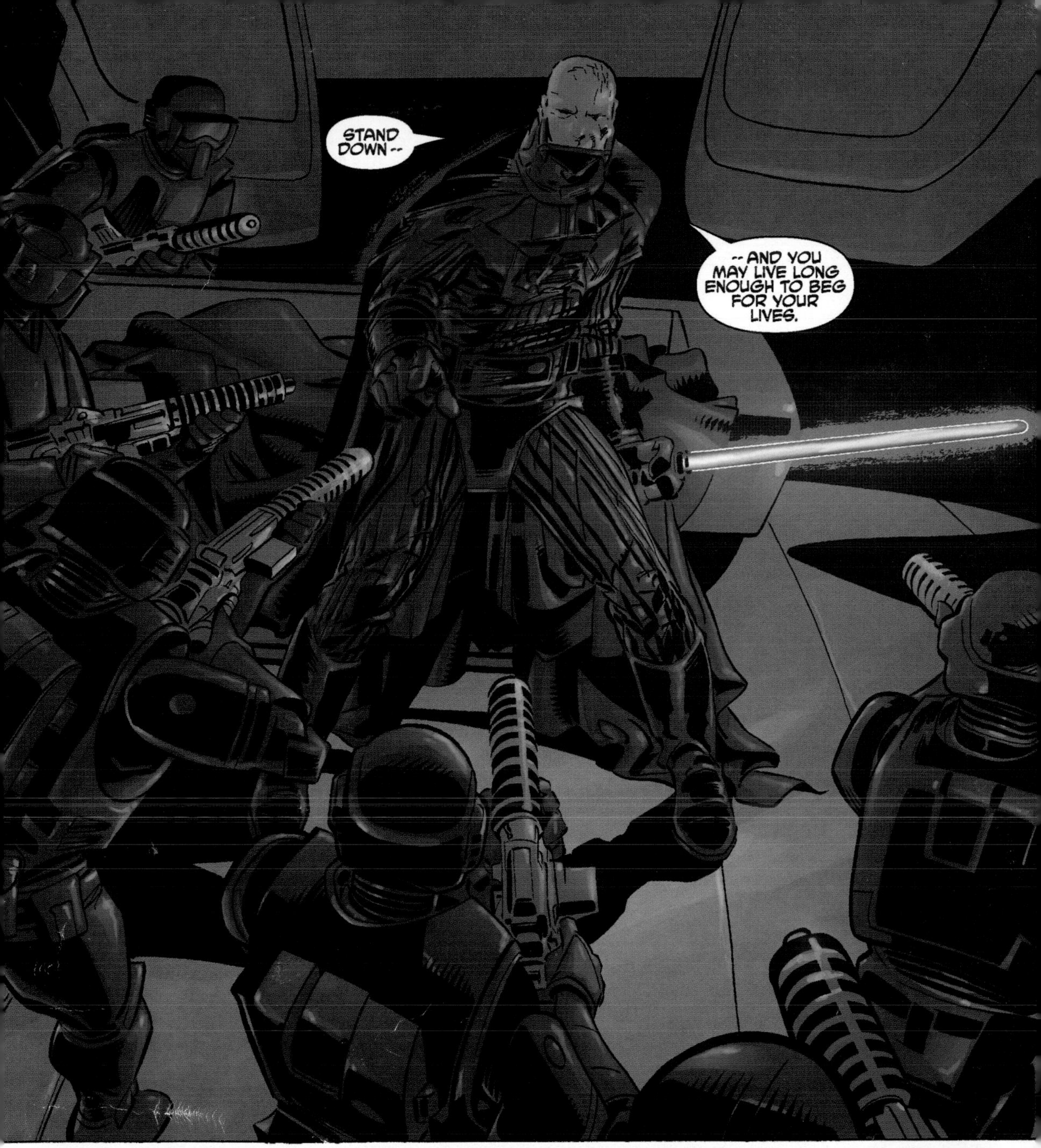
STAND DOWN --
-- AND YOU MAY LIVE LONG ENOUGH TO BEG FOR YOUR LIVES.

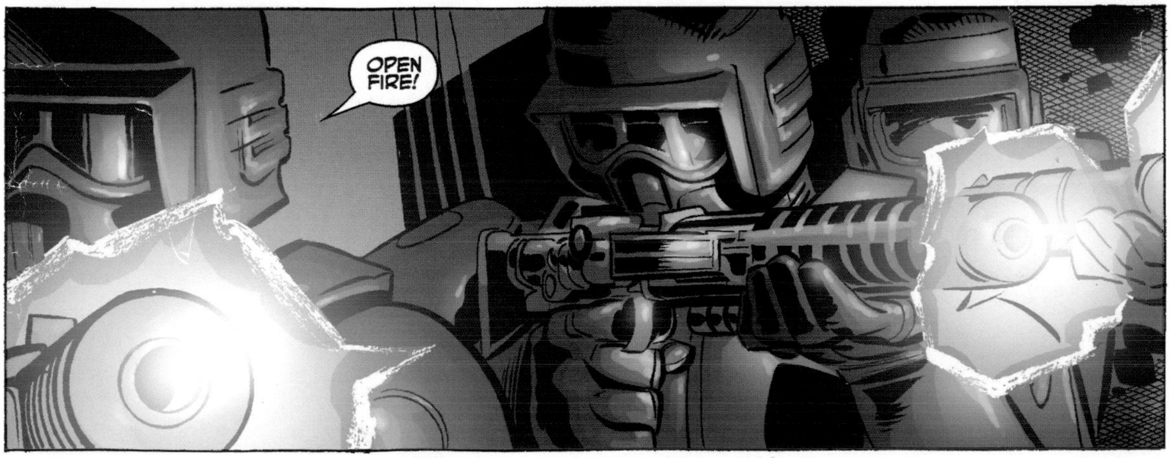
OPEN FIRE!

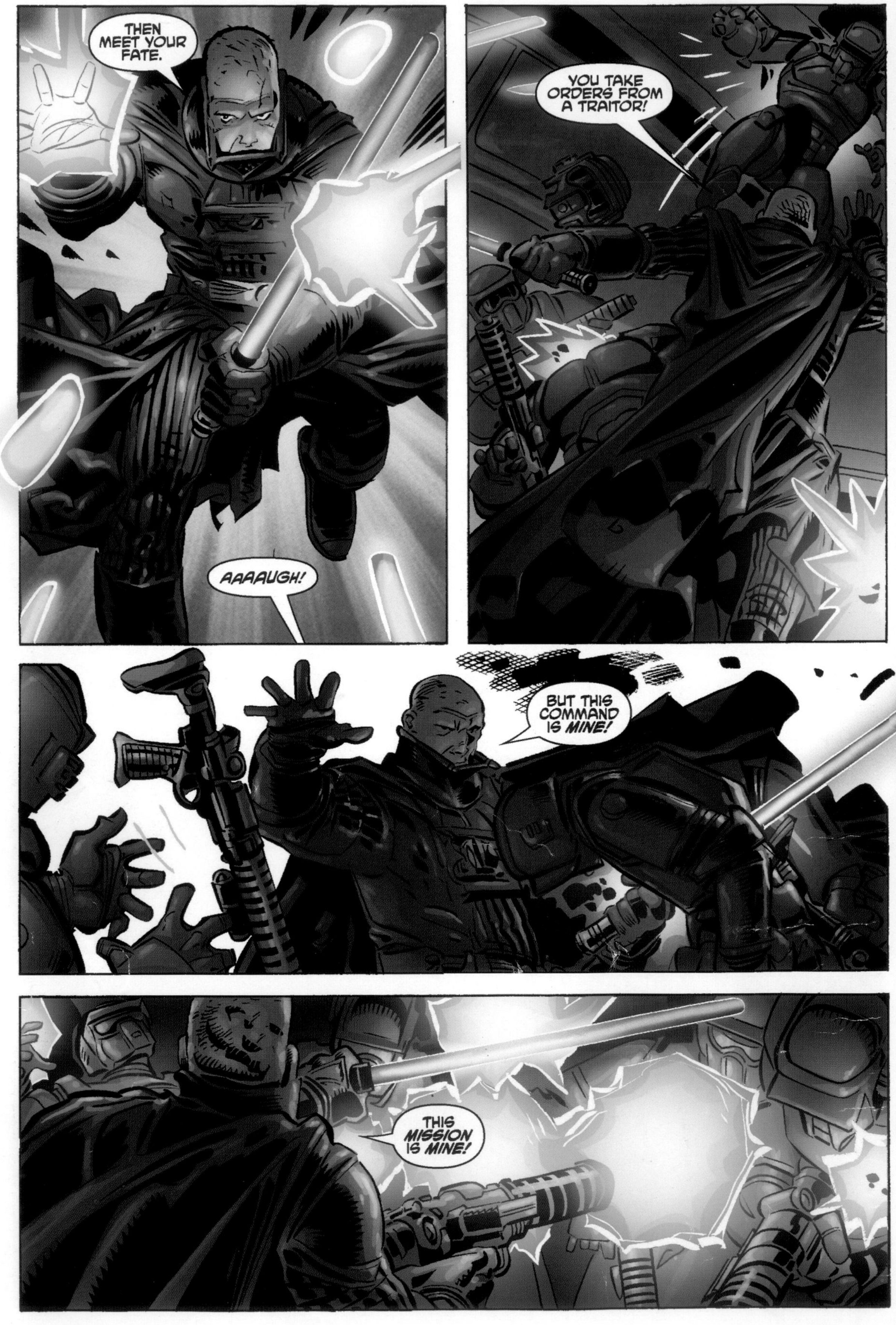
THEN MEET YOUR FATE.
AAAAUGH!
YOU TAKE ORDERS FROM A TRAITOR!
BUT THIS COMMAND IS *MINE!*
THIS *MISSION* IS *MINE!*

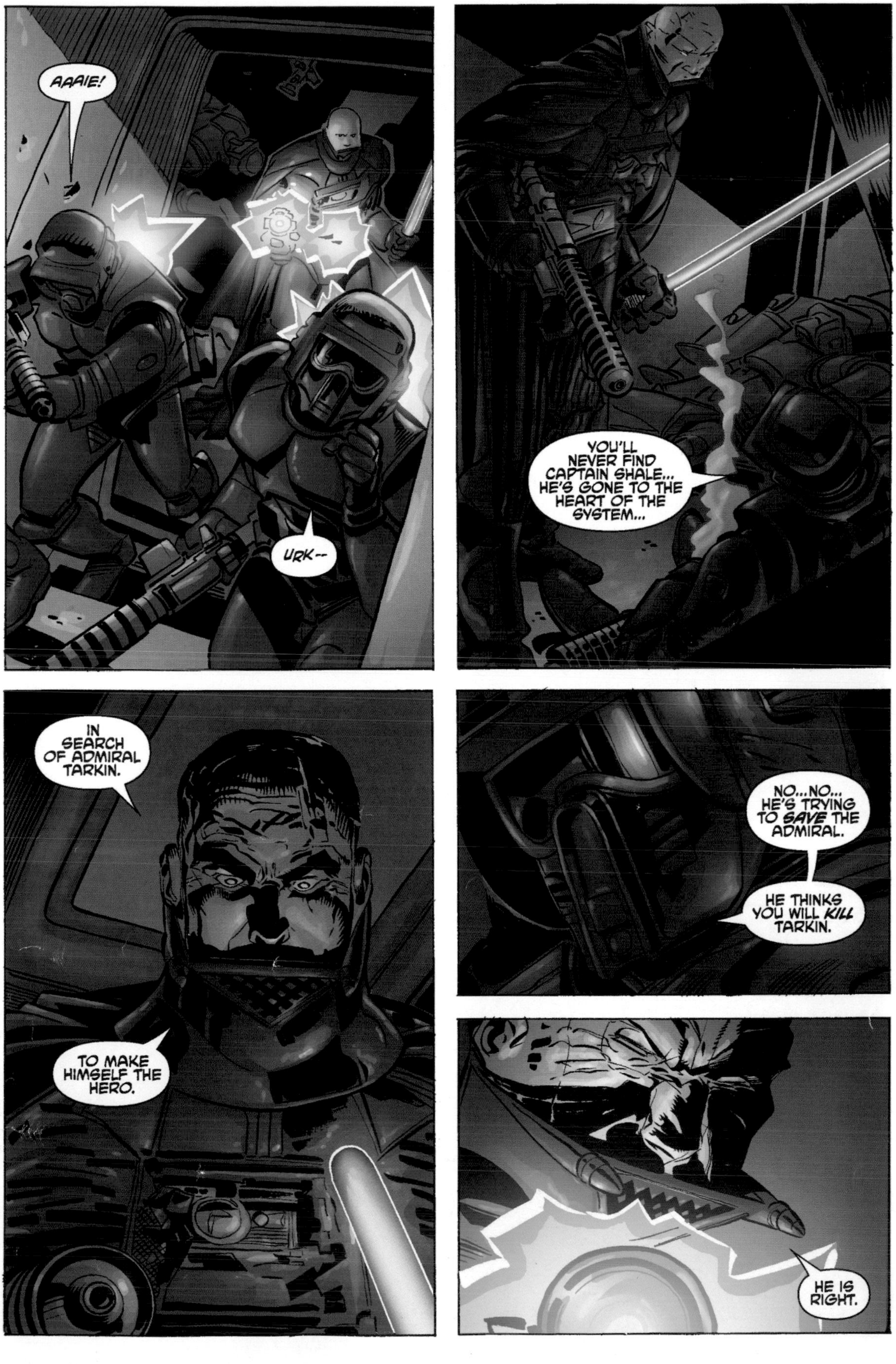
AAAIE!
URK--
YOU'LL NEVER FIND CAPTAIN SHALE... HE'S GONE TO THE HEART OF THE SYSTEM...
IN SEARCH OF ADMIRAL TARKIN.
TO MAKE HIMSELF THE HERO.
NO...NO... HE'S TRYING TO SAVE THE ADMIRAL.
HE THINKS YOU WILL KILL TARKIN.
HE IS RIGHT.

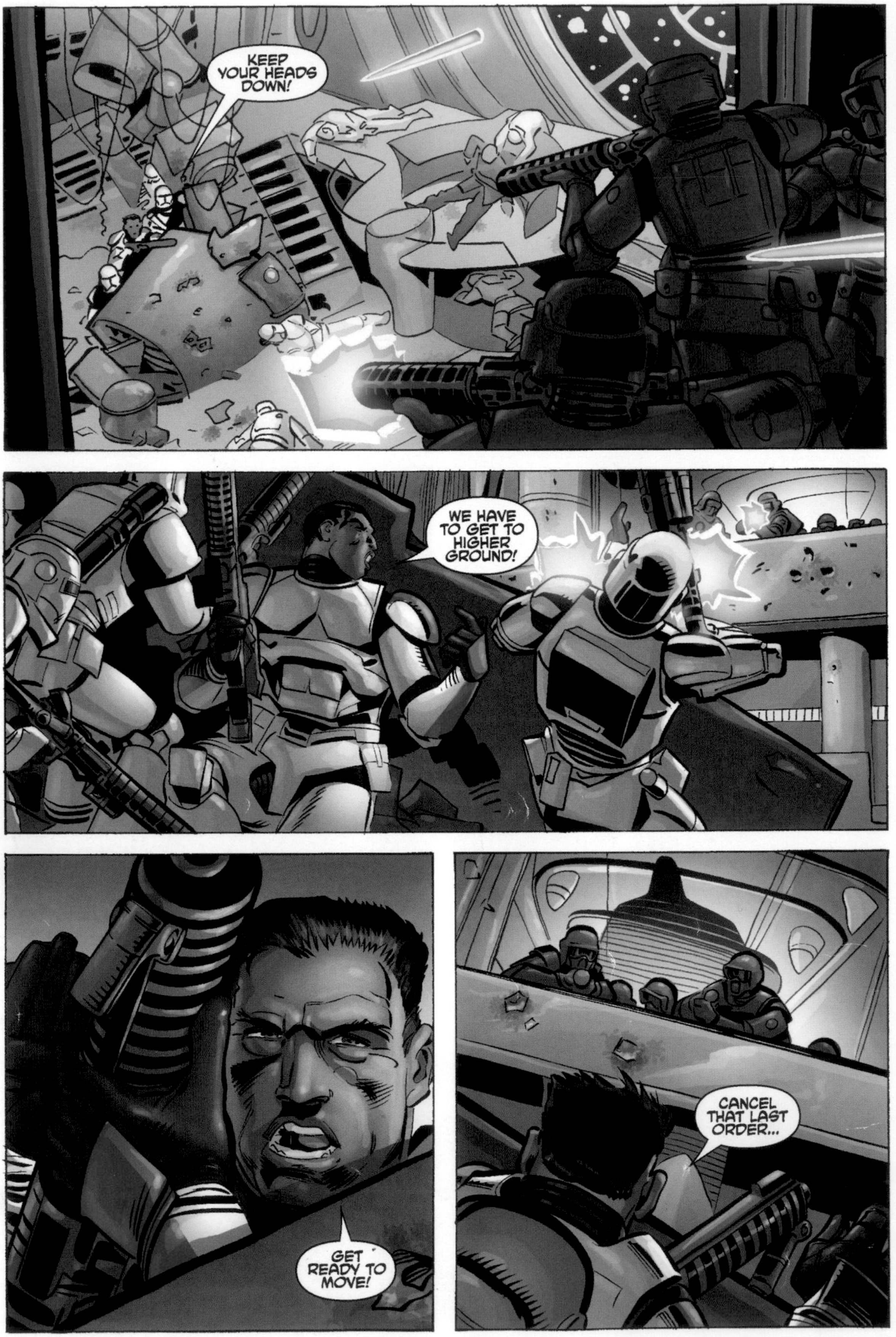
KEEP YOUR HEADS DOWN!
WE HAVE TO GET TO HIGHER GROUND!
GET READY TO MOVE!
CANCEL THAT LAST ORDER...

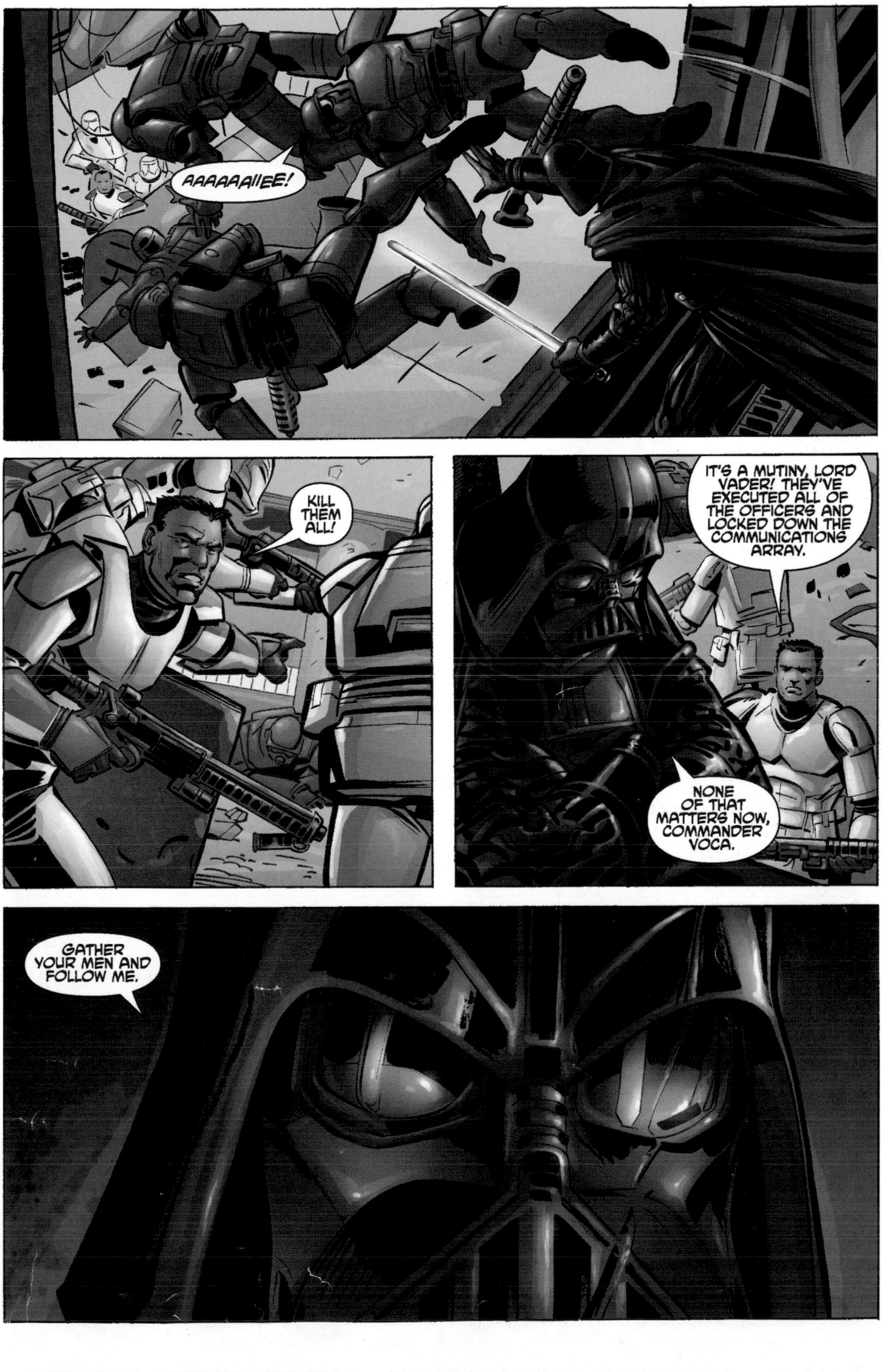
AAAAAAIIEE!
KILL THEM ALL!
IT'S A MUTINY, LORD VADER! THEY'VE EXECUTED ALL OF THE OFFICERS AND LOCKED DOWN THE COMMUNICATIONS ARRAY.
NONE OF THAT MATTERS NOW, COMMANDER VOCA.
GATHER YOUR MEN AND FOLLOW ME.

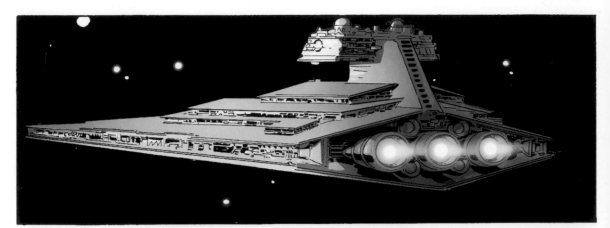

SEND YOUR ENGINEERS TO SHALE'S HANGAR AND ACTIVATE THE TRACKING DE--

BOOOOOM!

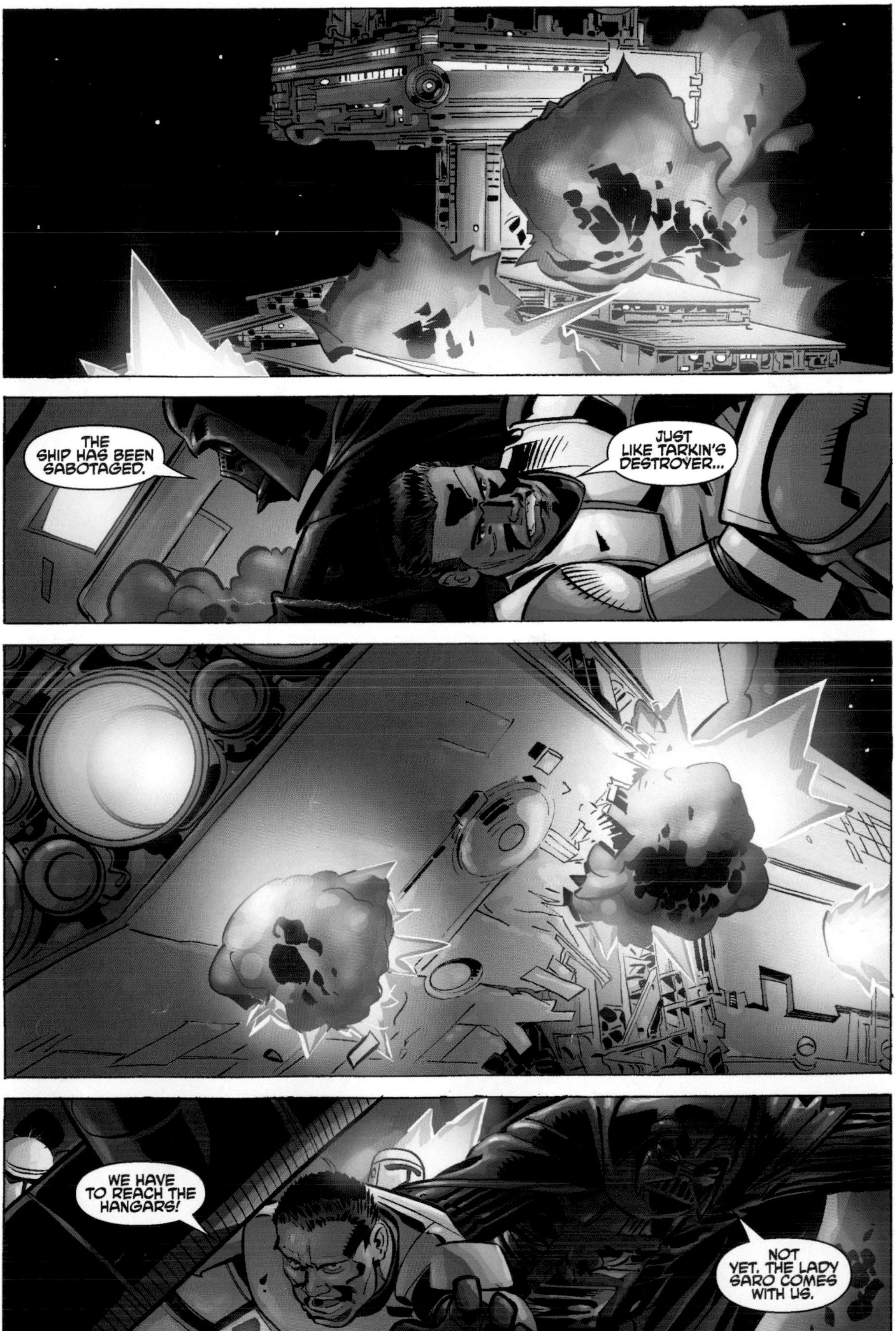
THE SHIP HAS BEEN SABOTAGED.
JUST LIKE TARKIN'S DESTROYER...
WE HAVE TO REACH THE HANGARS!
NOT YET. THE LADY SARO COMES WITH US.

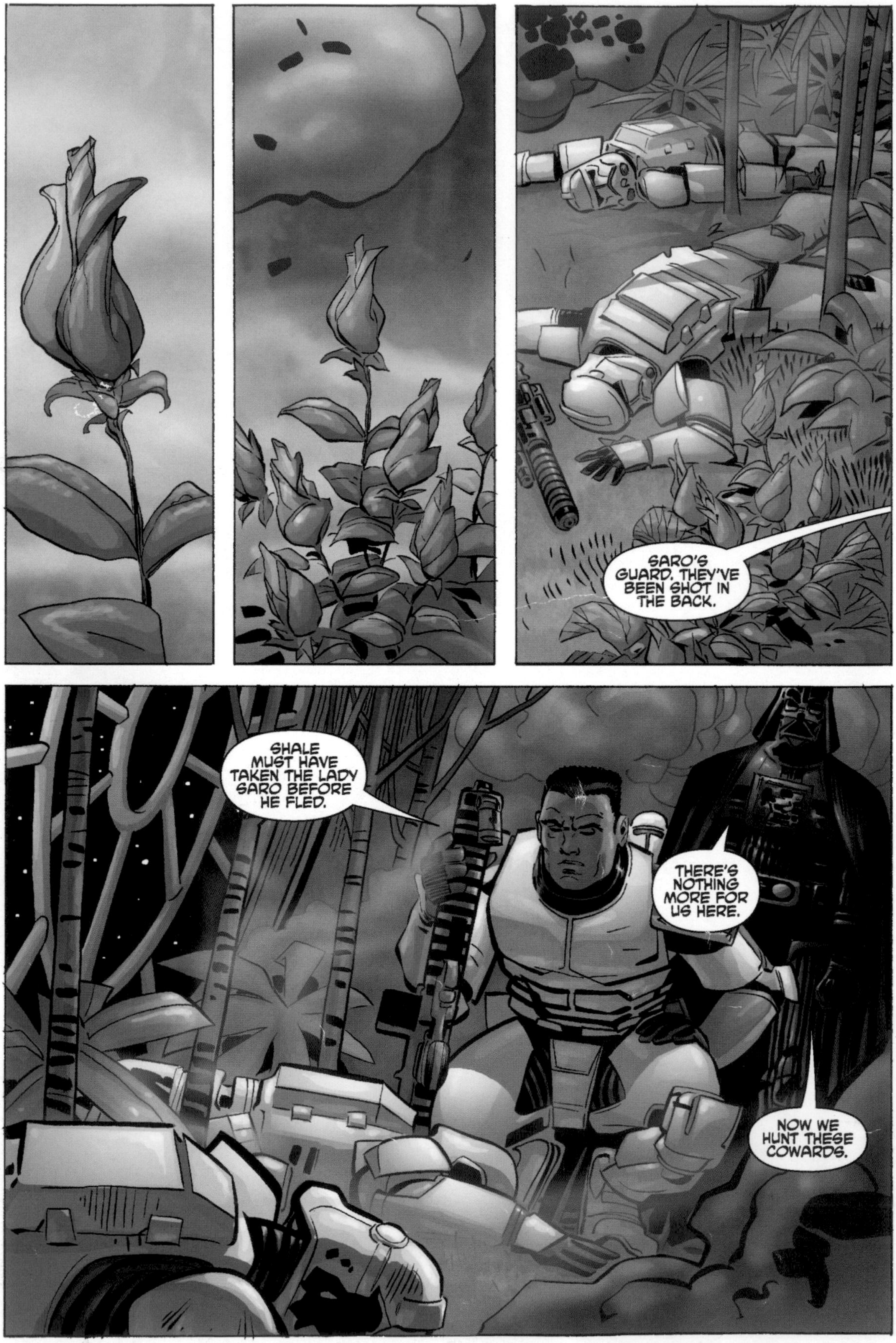
SARO'S GUARD. THEY'VE BEEN SHOT IN THE BACK.
SHALE MUST HAVE TAKEN THE LADY SARO BEFORE HE FLED.
THERE'S NOTHING MORE FOR US HERE.
NOW WE HUNT THESE COWARDS.

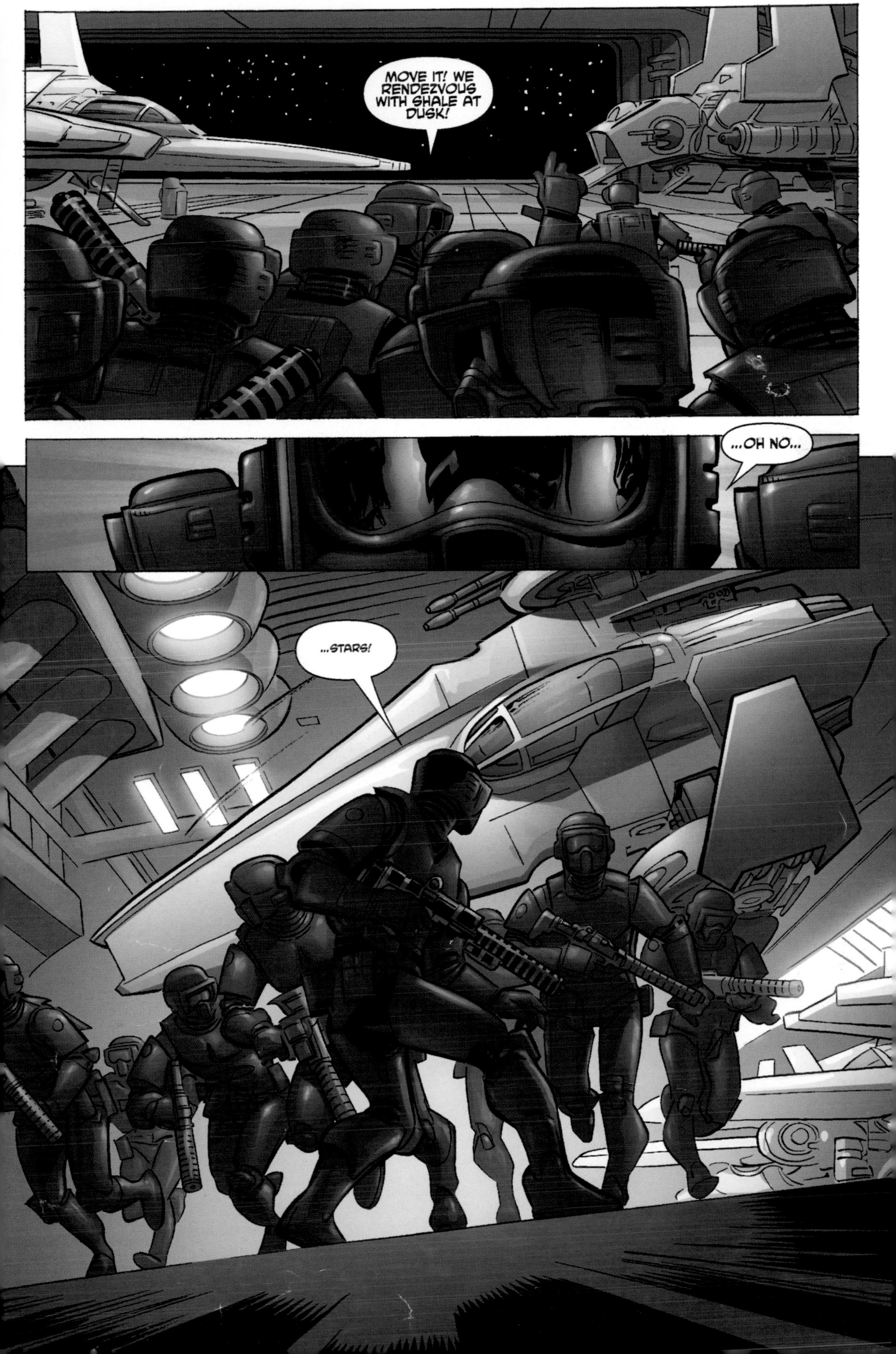
MOVE IT! WE RENDEZVOUS WITH SHALE AT DUSK!
...OH NO...
...STARS!

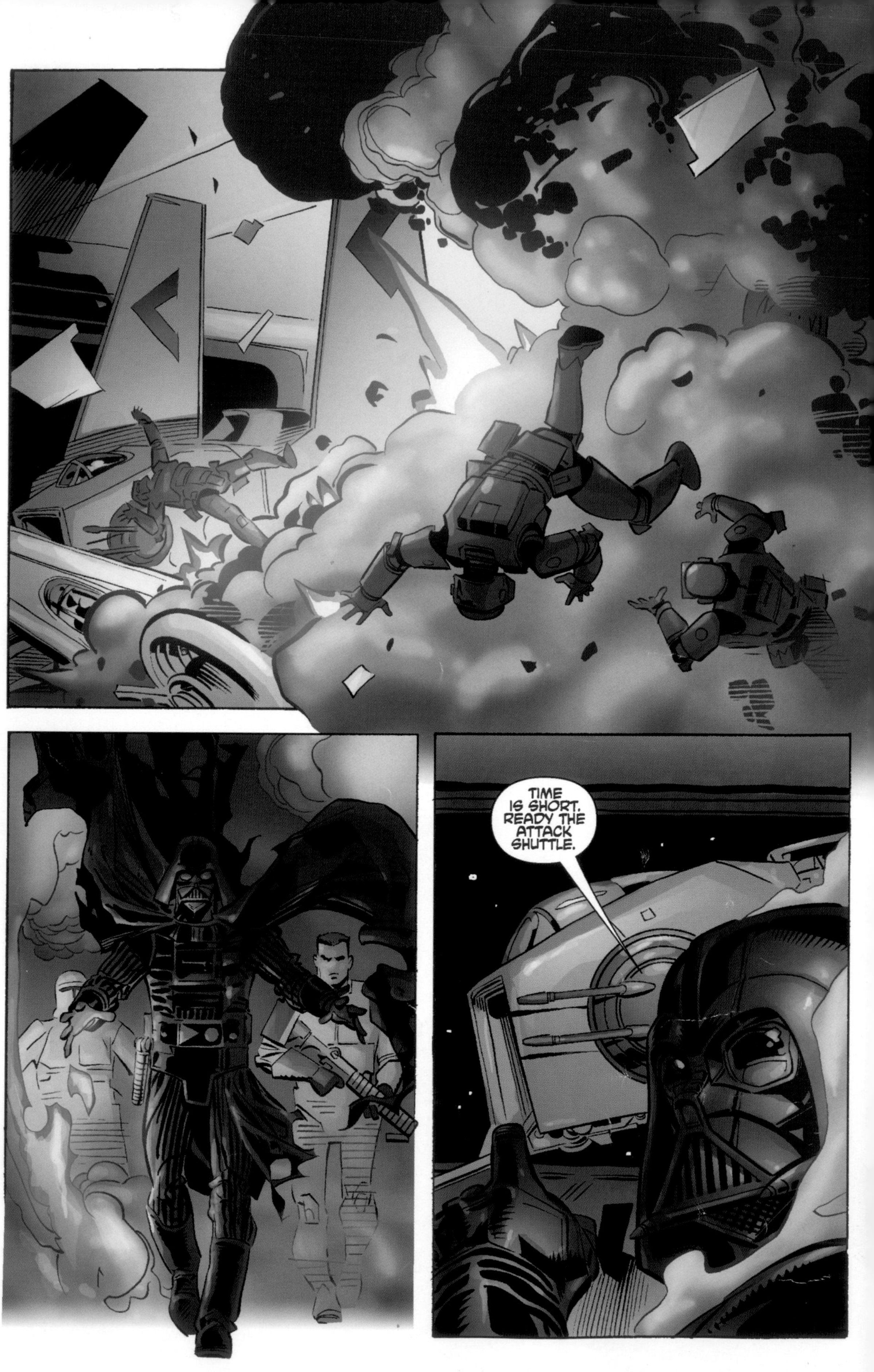
TIME IS SHORT. READY THE ATTACK SHUTTLE.

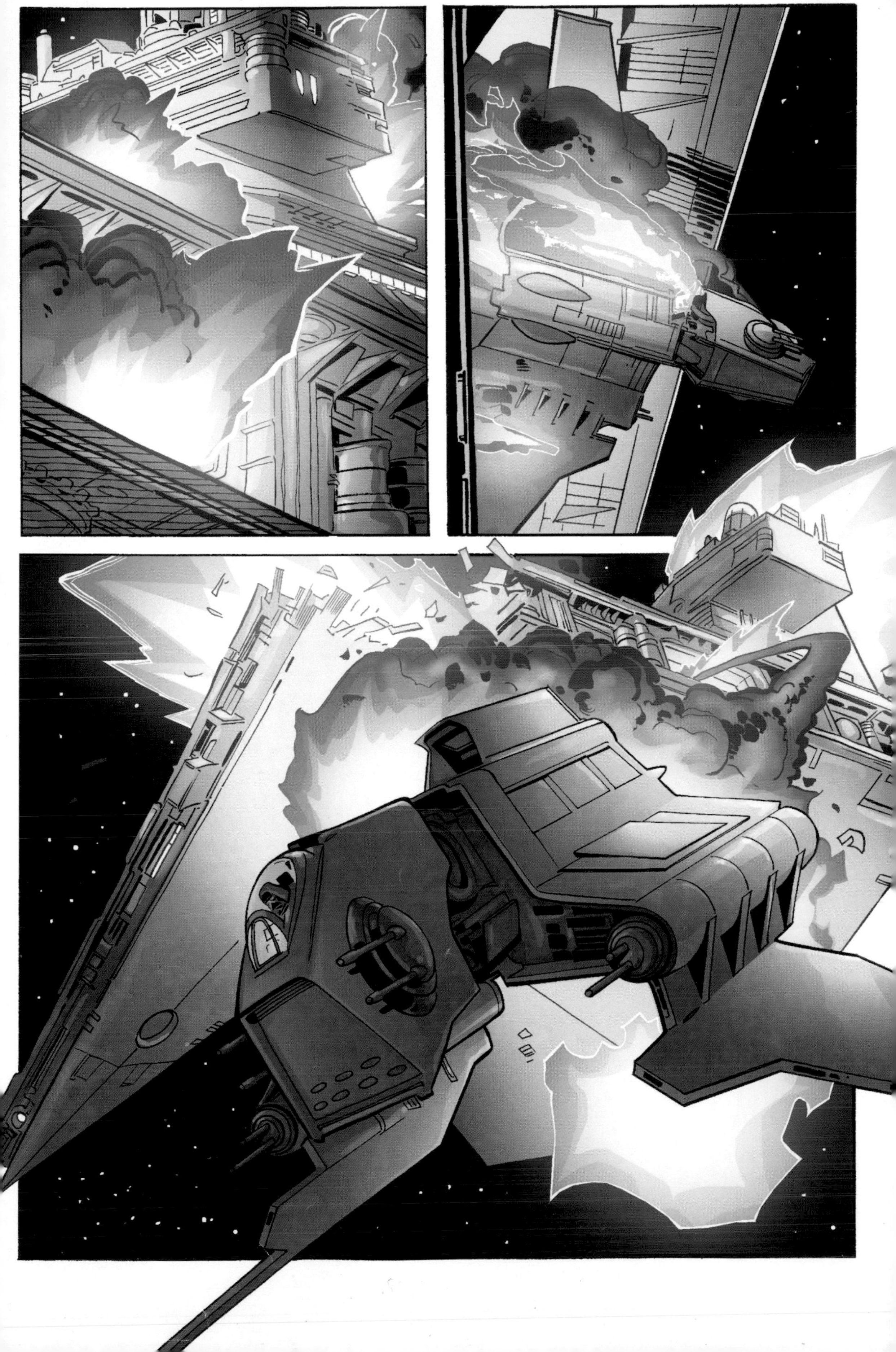

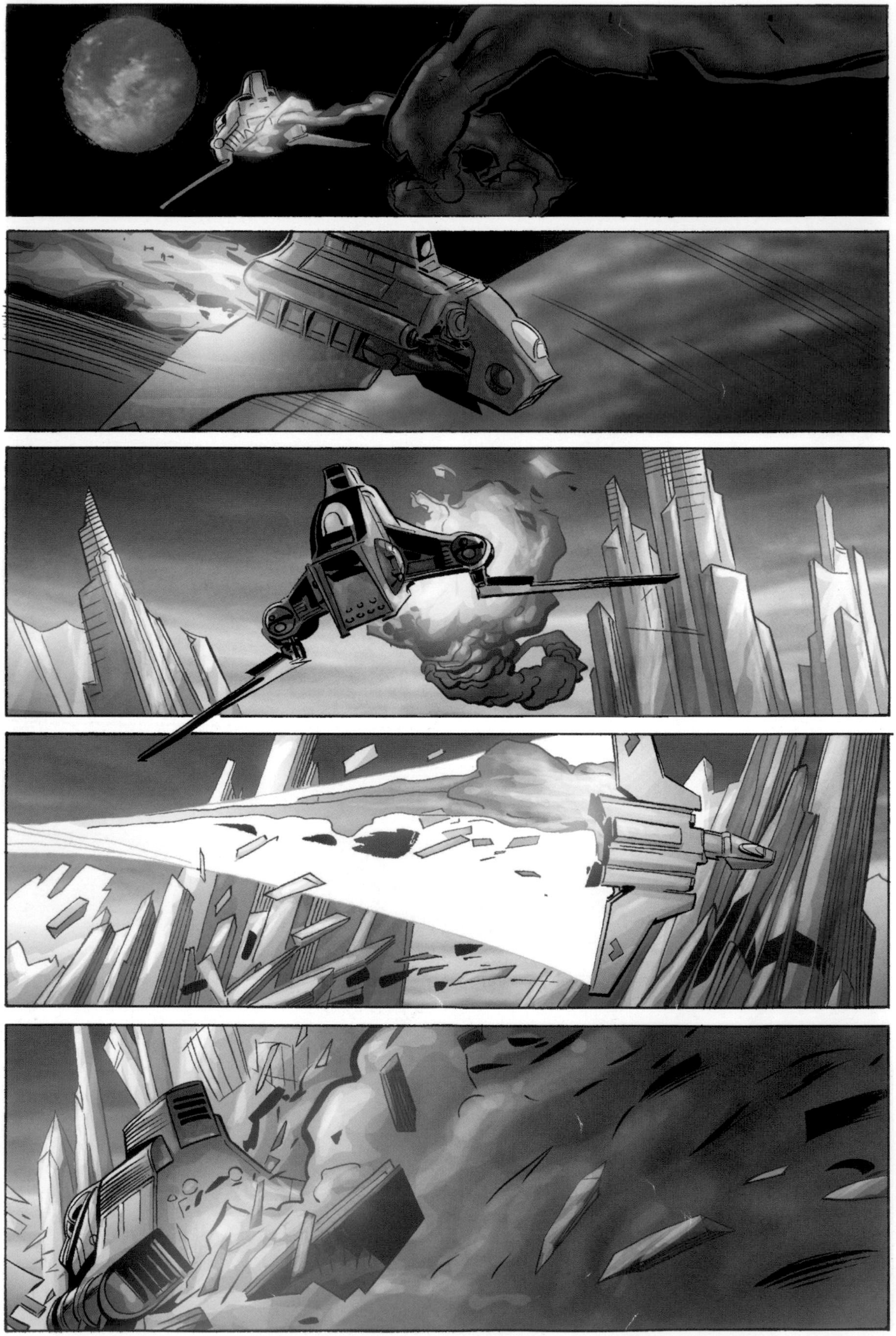

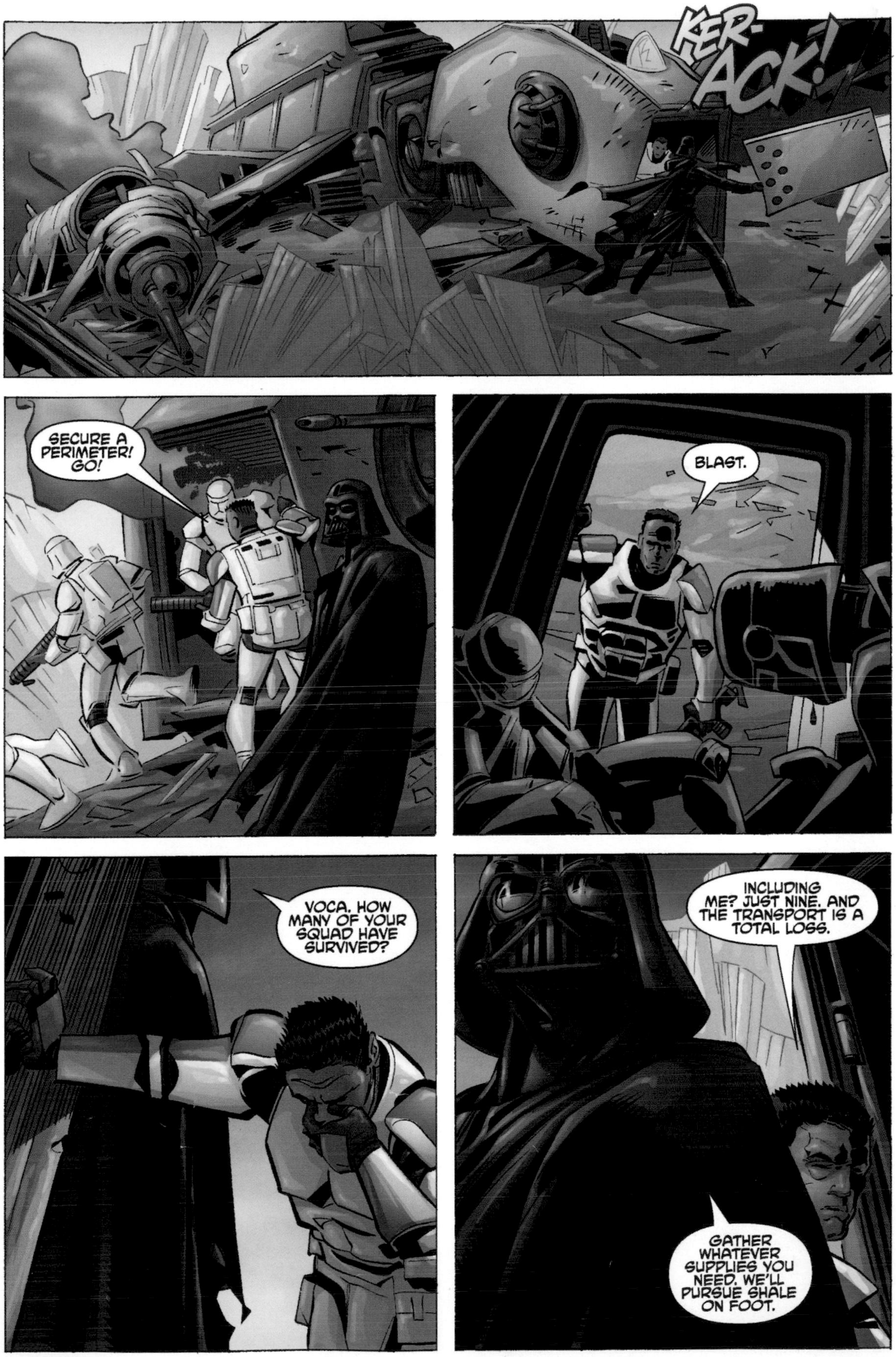
KER-ACK!
SECURE A PERIMETER! GO!
BLAST.
VOCA. HOW MANY OF YOUR SQUAD HAVE SURVIVED?
INCLUDING ME? JUST NINE. AND THE TRANSPORT IS A TOTAL LOSS.
GATHER WHATEVER SUPPLIES YOU NEED. WE'LL PURSUE SHALE ON FOOT.

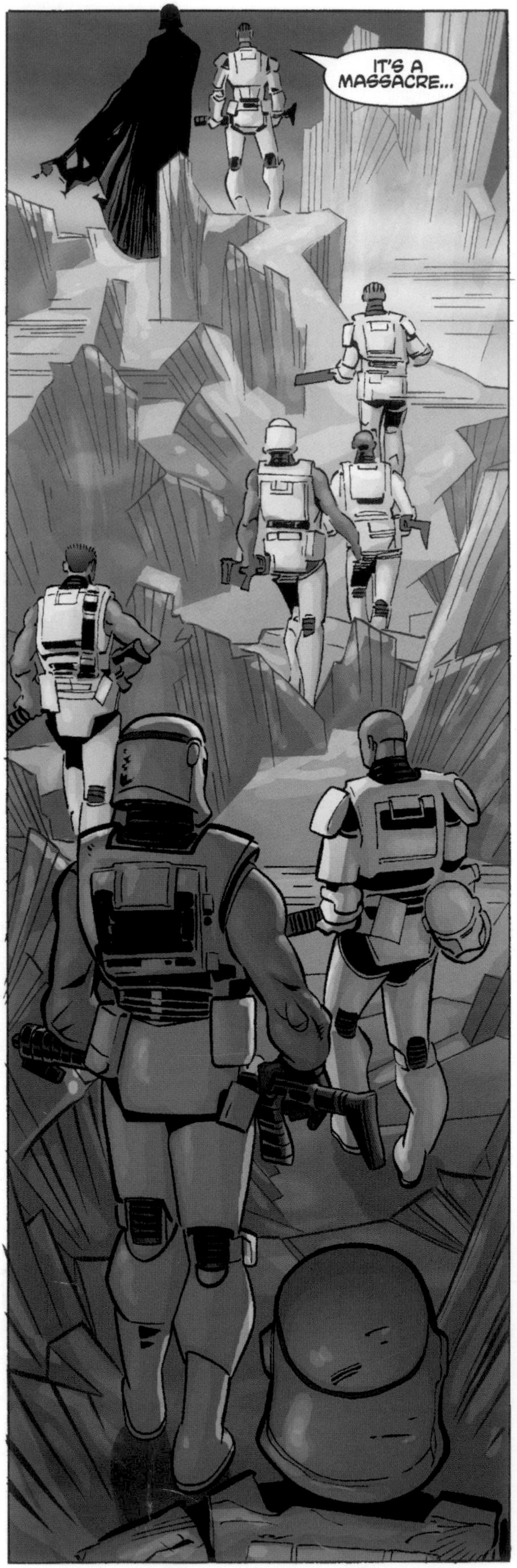
IT'S A MASSACRE...

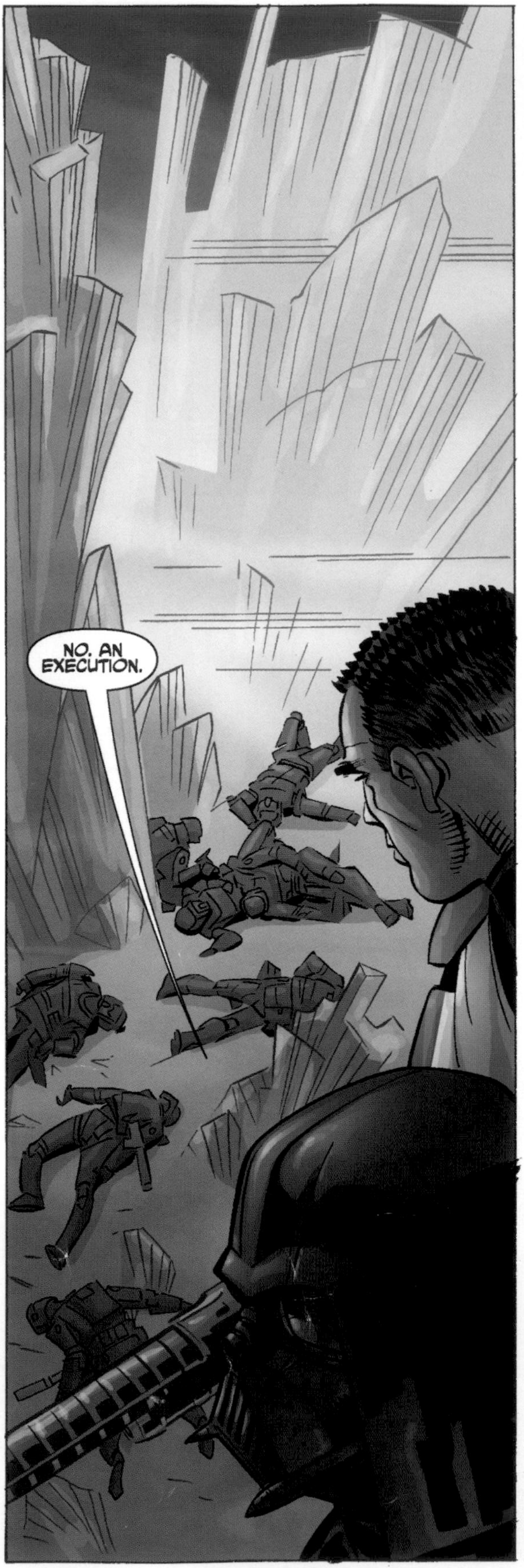
NO. AN EXECUTION.

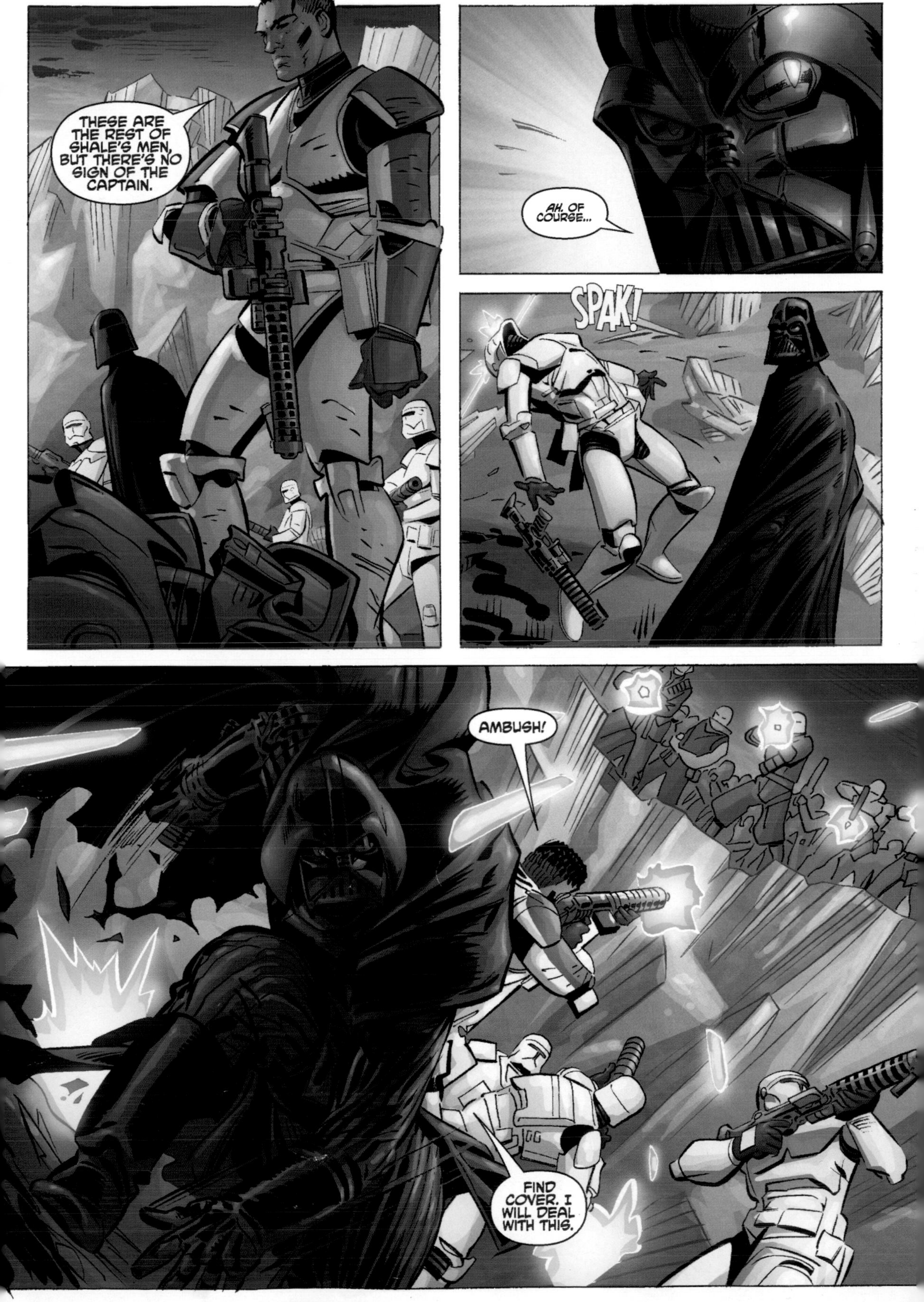
THESE ARE THE REST OF SHALE'S MEN, BUT THERE'S NO SIGN OF THE CAPTAIN.
AH. OF COURSE...
SPAK!
AMBUSH!
FIND COVER. I WILL DEAL WITH THIS.

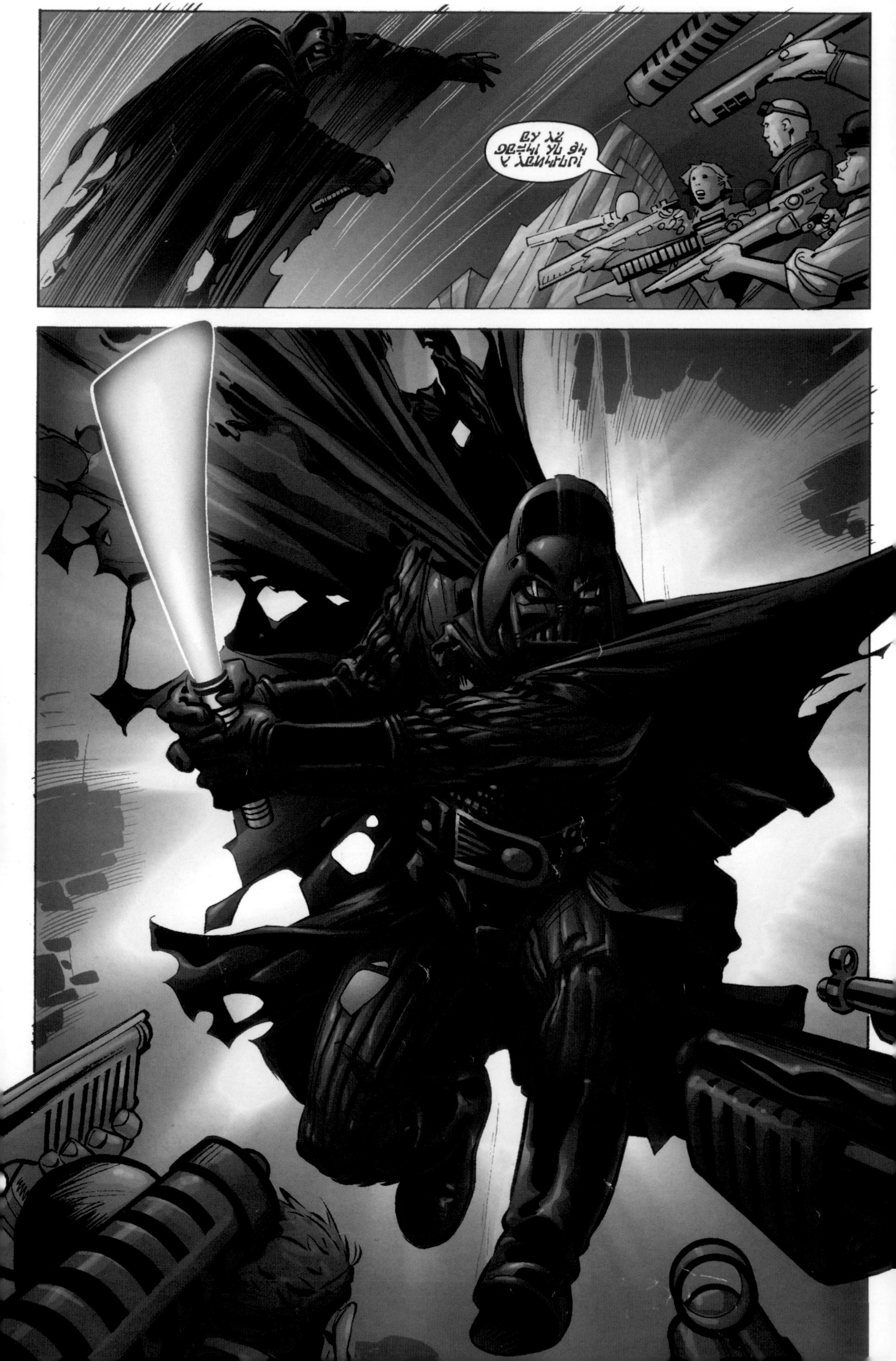

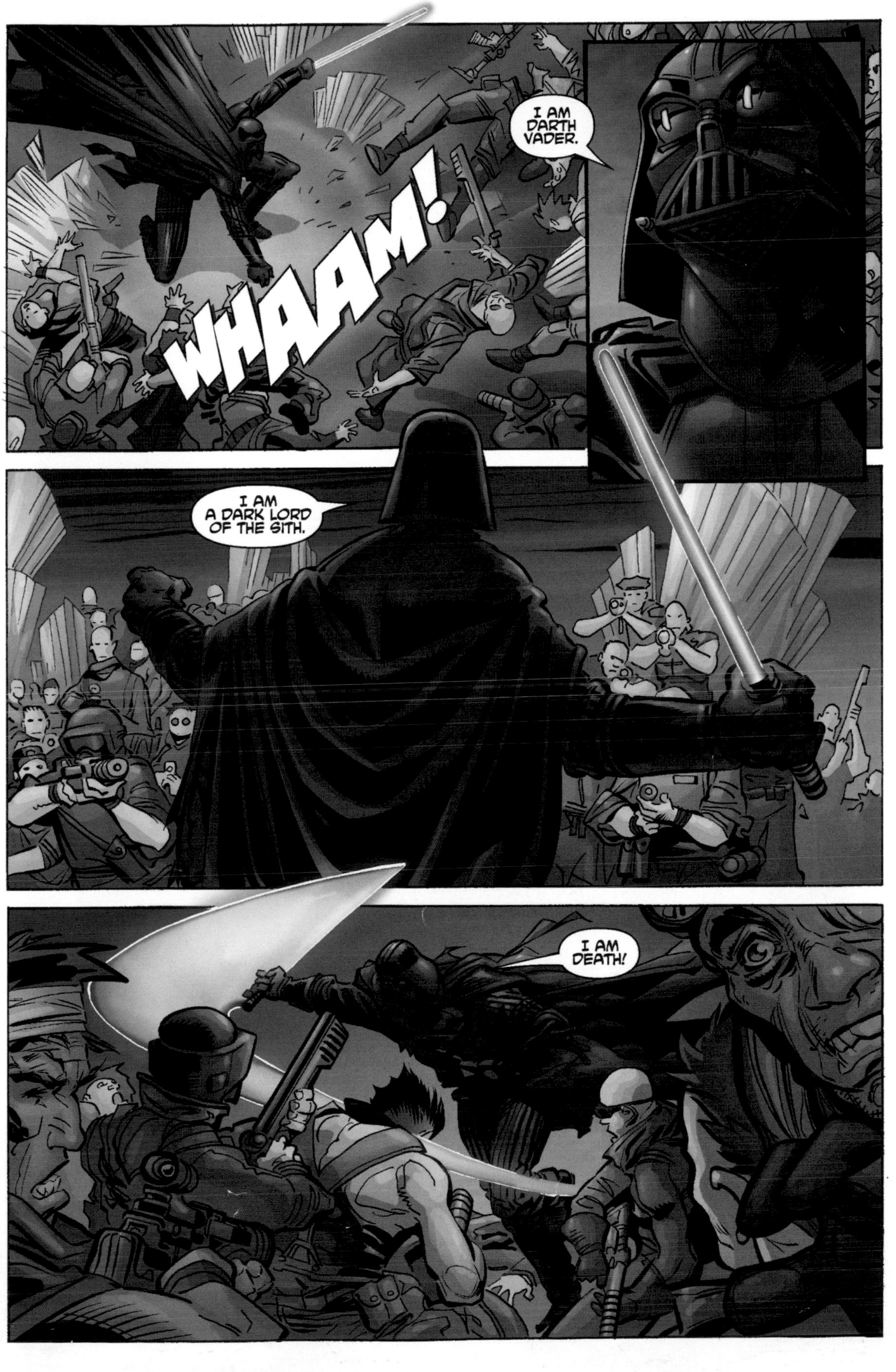
WHAAM!
I AM DARTH VADER.
I AM A DARK LORD OF THE SITH.
I AM DEATH!

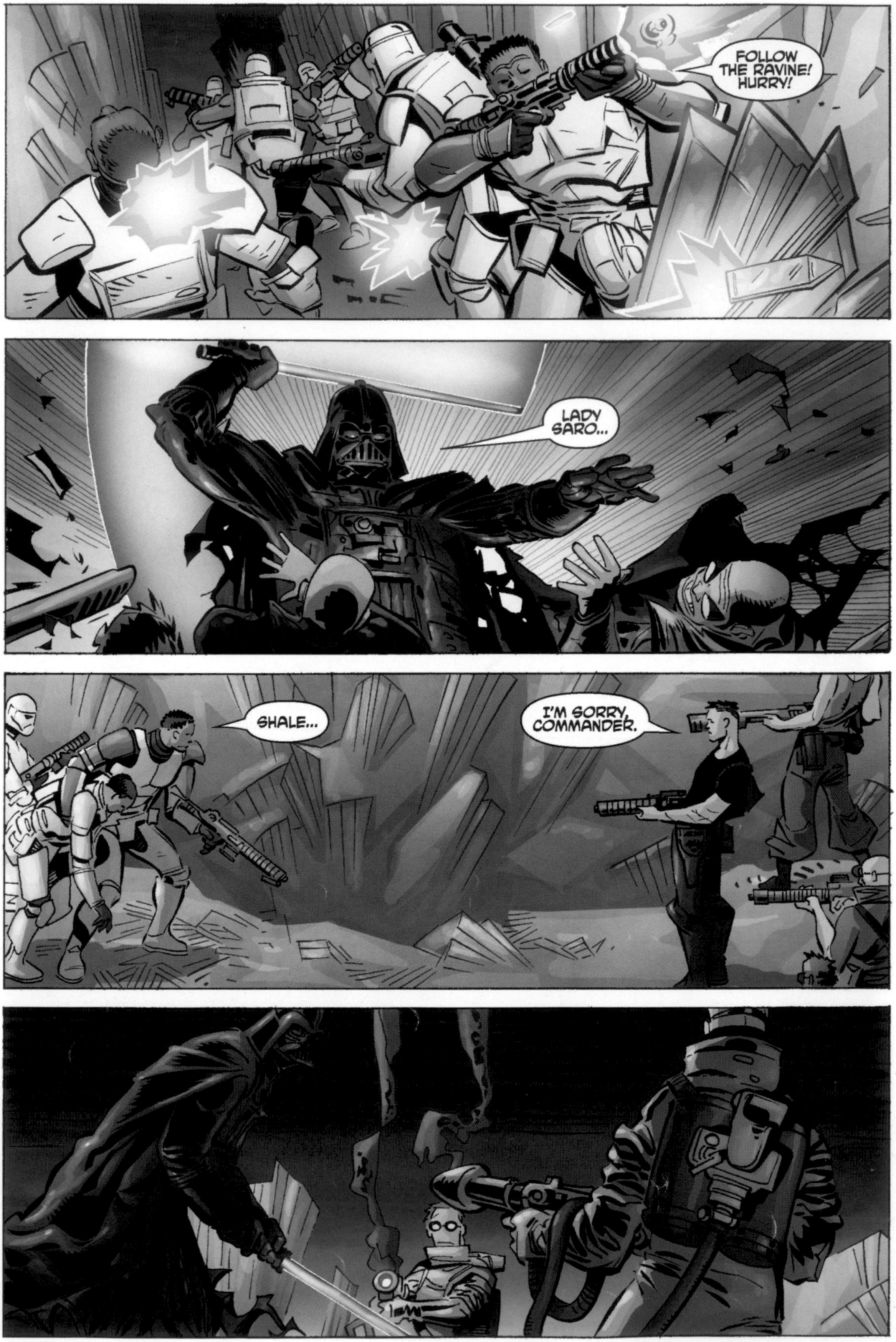
FOLLOW THE RAVINE! HURRY!
LADY SARO...
SHALE...
I'M SORRY, COMMANDER.

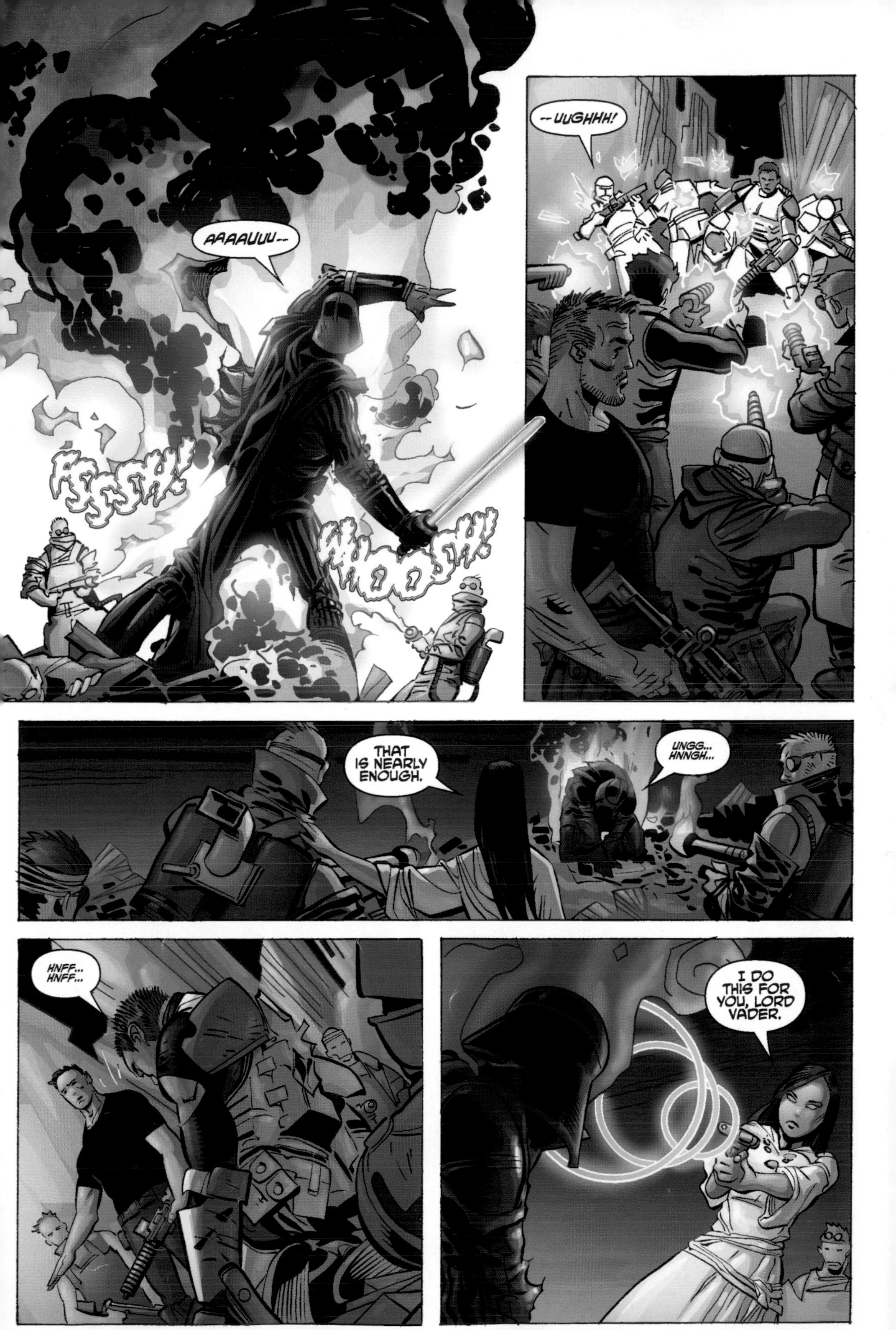
AAAAUUU--
FSSSH!
WHOOSH!
--UUGHHH!
THAT IS NEARLY ENOUGH.
UNGG... HNNGH...
HNFF... HNFF...
I DO THIS FOR YOU, LORD VADER.

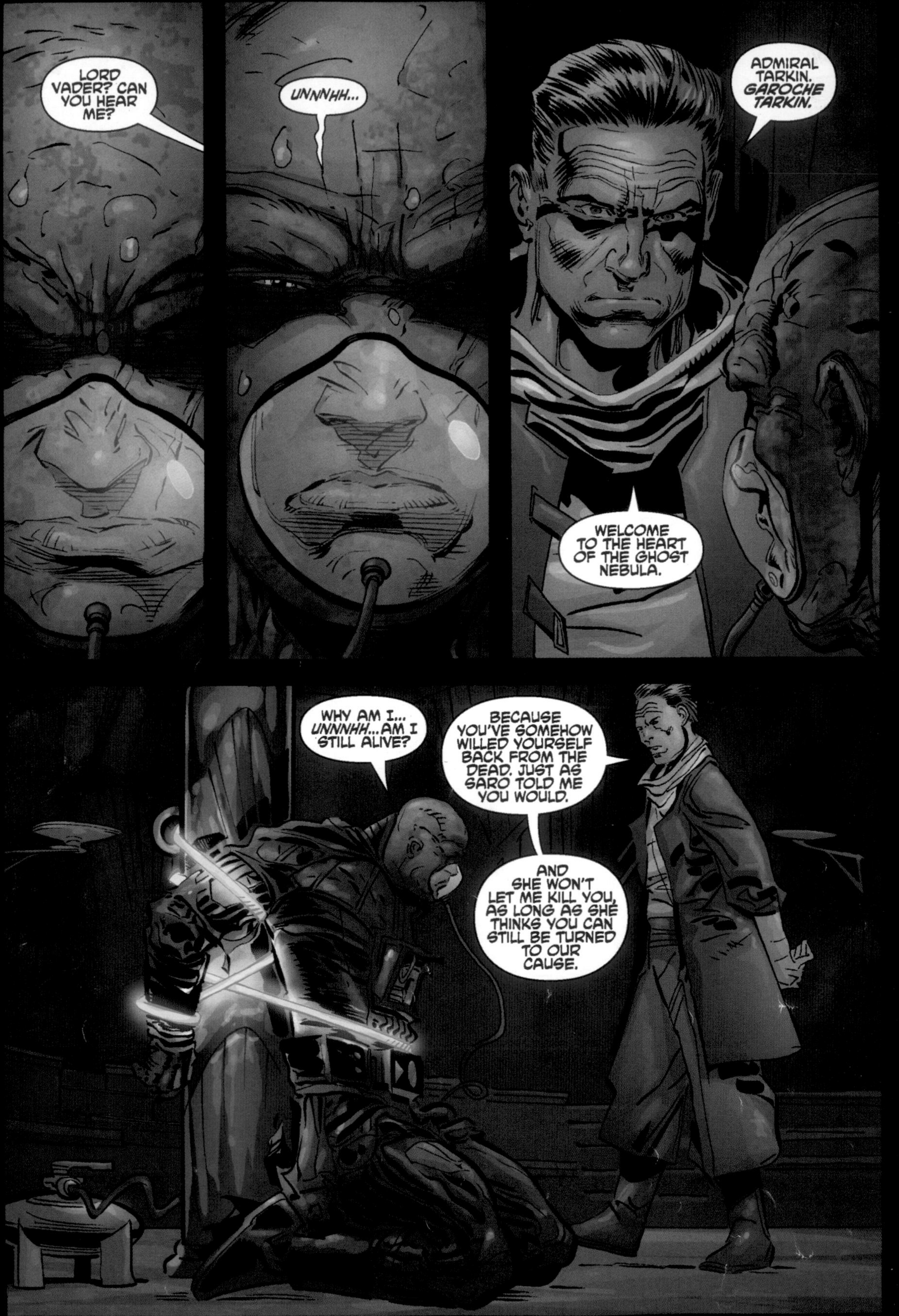
LORD VADER? CAN YOU HEAR ME?
UNNNHH...
ADMIRAL TARKIN. GAROCHE TARKIN.
WELCOME TO THE HEART OF THE GHOST NEBULA.
WHY AM I... UNNNHH... AM I STILL ALIVE?
BECAUSE YOU'VE SOMEHOW WILLED YOURSELF BACK FROM THE DEAD. JUST AS SARO TOLD ME YOU WOULD.
AND SHE WON'T LET ME KILL YOU, AS LONG AS SHE THINKS YOU CAN STILL BE TURNED TO OUR CAUSE.

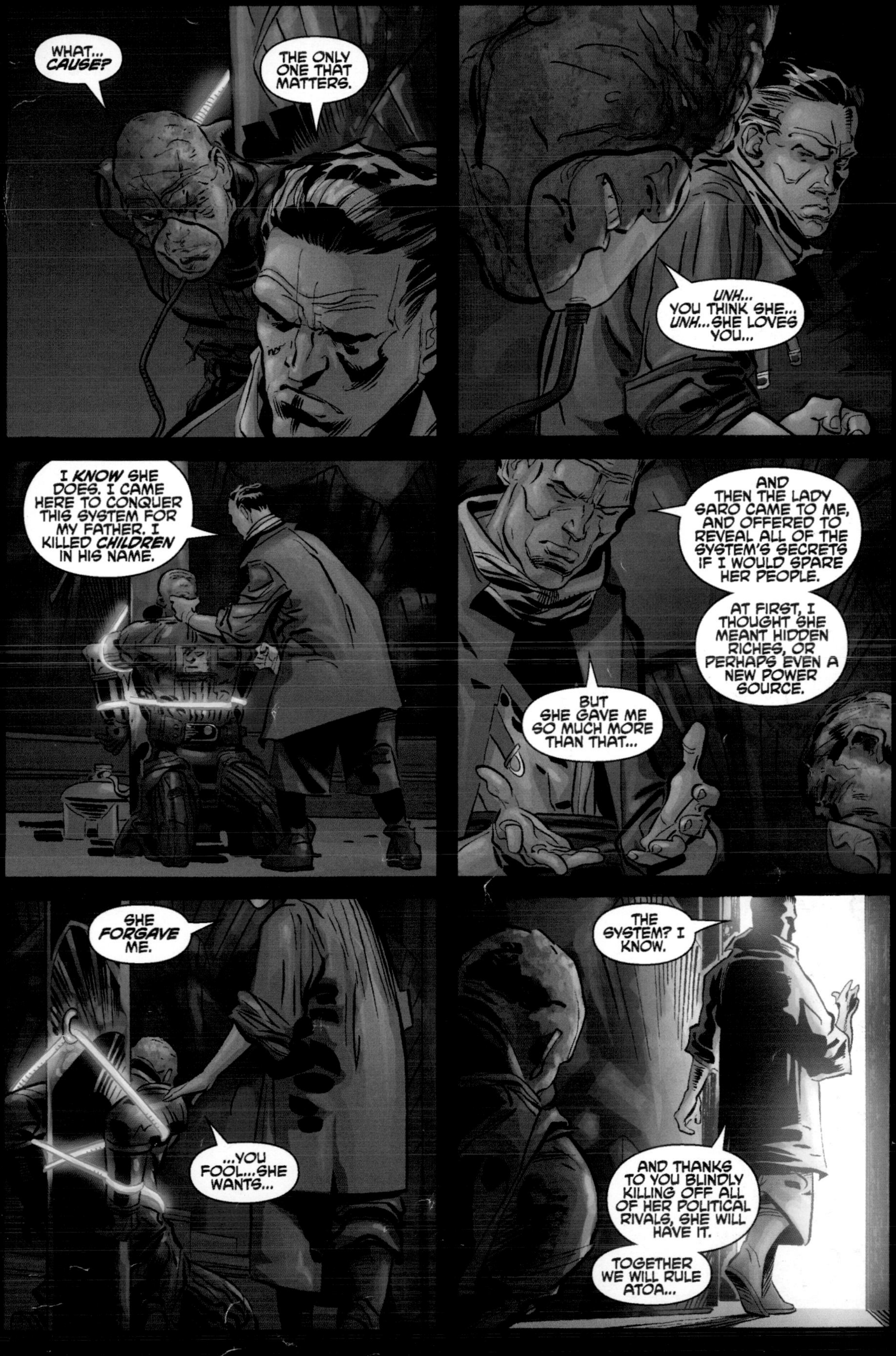

WHAT... *CAUSE?*
THE ONLY ONE THAT MATTERS.
UNH... YOU THINK SHE... *UNH...* SHE LOVES YOU...
I *KNOW* SHE DOES. I CAME HERE TO CONQUER THIS SYSTEM FOR MY FATHER. I KILLED *CHILDREN* IN HIS NAME.
AND THEN THE LADY SARO CAME TO ME, AND OFFERED TO REVEAL ALL OF THE SYSTEM'S SECRETS IF I WOULD SPARE HER PEOPLE.
AT FIRST, I THOUGHT SHE MEANT HIDDEN RICHES, OR PERHAPS EVEN A NEW POWER SOURCE.
BUT SHE GAVE ME SO MUCH MORE THAN THAT...
SHE *FORGAVE* ME.
...YOU FOOL... SHE WANTS...
THE SYSTEM? I KNOW.
AND THANKS TO YOU BLINDLY KILLING OFF ALL OF HER POLITICAL RIVALS, SHE WILL HAVE IT.
TOGETHER WE WILL RULE ATOA...

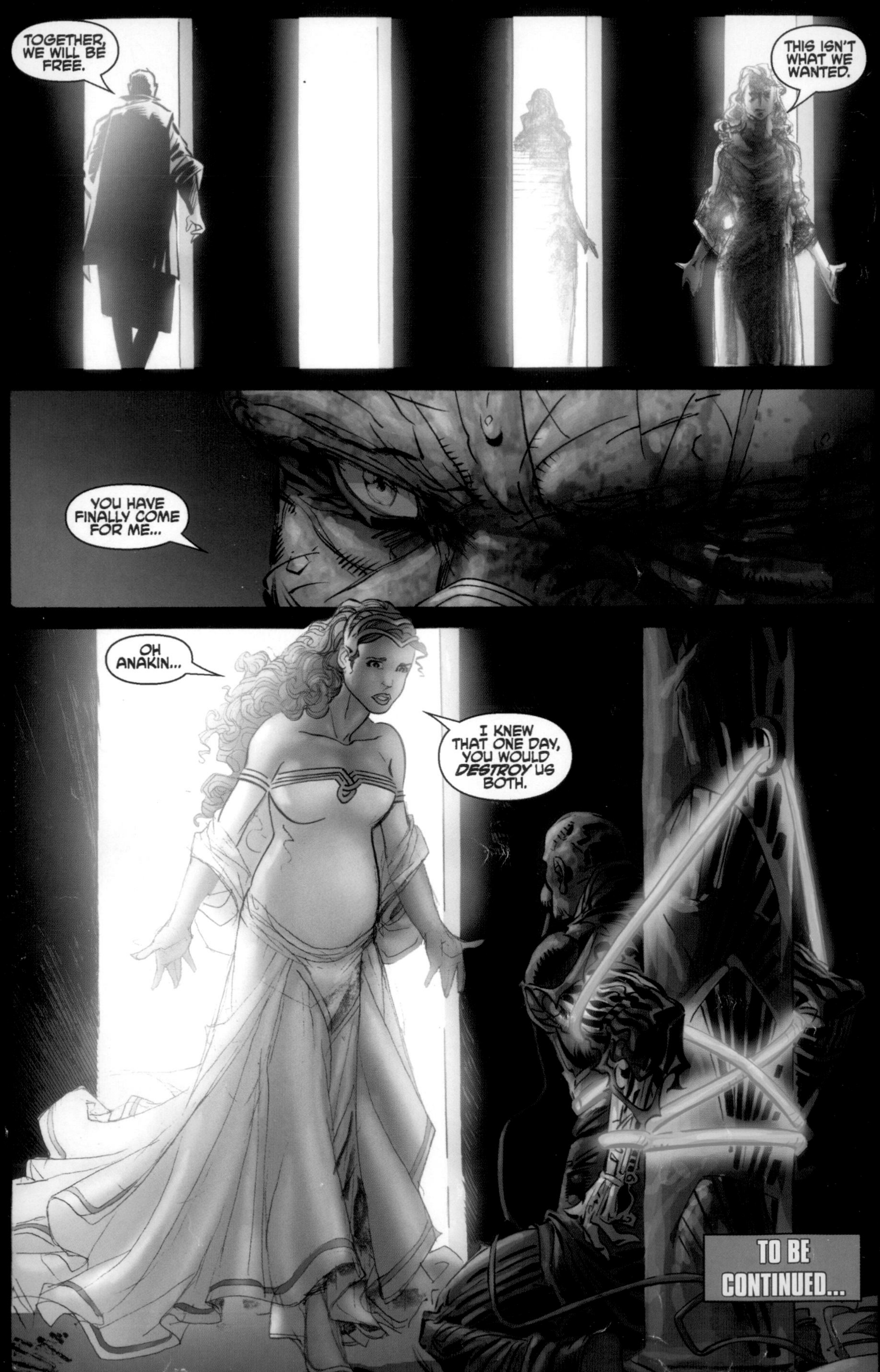
TOGETHER, WE WILL BE FREE.
THIS ISN'T WHAT WE WANTED.
YOU HAVE FINALLY COME FOR ME...
OH ANAKIN...
I KNEW THAT ONE DAY, YOU WOULD DESTROY US BOTH.
TO BE CONTINUED...